OK OUT FOR THE WHOLE SERIES!

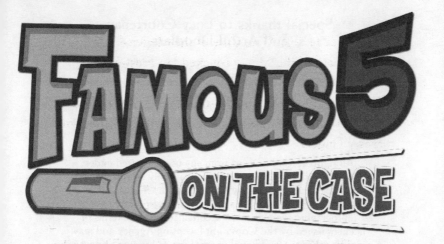

THE CASE OF THE FLOWERS THAT
MAKE YOUR BODY ALL WOBBLY

Hodder
Children's
Books

A division of Hachette Children's Books

Special thanks to Lucy Courtenay
and Artful Doodlers

Copyright © 2009 Chorion Rights Limited, a Chorion company

First published in Great Britain in 2009 by Hodder Children's Books

3

A Catalogue record for this book is available from the British Library

ISBN 978 0 340 97086 7

Typeset in Weiss by Avon DataSet Ltd,
Bidford on Avon, Warwickshire

Printed and bound in Great Britain by
Clays Ltd, St Ives plc

The paper and board used in this paperback by Hodder Children's
Books are natural recyclable products made from wood grown in
sustainable forests. The manufacturing processes conform to the
environmental regulations of the country of origin.

Hodder Children's Books
a division of Hachette Children's Books
338 Euston Road, London NW1 3BH
An Hachette Livre UK Company
www.hachettelivre.co.uk

Chapter One

A warm afternoon breeze ruffled the linen cloths that covered the tables in the garden. The members of the Falcongate Rose Society chattered excitedly and helped themselves to the buffet. It wasn't every day that Falcongate saw an event as grand as this, and the guests were making the most of it.

As it was her mother George's party, Jo and her three Kirrin cousins were making themselves useful by being waiters. Jo and Allie were doing their best to keep the glasses topped up and the guests happy. The boys, however, weren't taking their jobs very seriously at all.

Over at the buffet table, Max straightened his

black bow-tie, tucked in his white shirt, brushed his blond fringe out of his eyes and helped himself to a walnut from the nut selection. Dylan picked up a baguette and swung it round like a cricket bat. He pushed his glasses up his nose and narrowed his eyes at his cousin. Or, more specifically, at the walnut.

Before Max had a chance to pitch the walnut at Dylan, Allie bustled past. Her bow-tie and white shirt were immaculate. Holding a tray of

canapés up high, she moved between the guests, straightening the cloths.

"Tsk-tsk," she said briskly, stopping at a table. "Unfolded napkin."

She shifted her tray to the other hand and folded the wonky napkin into a swan with a flick of her wrist. Satisfied, she marched on towards one of the Falcongate Rose Society's well-known members.

"Vol-au-vent, Constable Stubblefield?" she said politely, waving the tray under the nose of Falcongate's large, romance-novel-loving police constable.

Constable Stubblefield waggled her fingers and started tucking in to the little pastries. Then, when she couldn't pick up as many as she wanted, the constable took the entire tray out of Allie's hands. It seemed easier that way.

Looking distracted, George stopped in front of Allie. She had a twig in her hair. Allie's aunt spent most of her time in her greenhouses with a collection of plants from around the world, so the twig was not unusual.

"When's your friend Courtney getting here?" George asked her niece.

Allie beamed at the mention of Courtney. "Her flight from LA already landed," she said. "I hope she gets here before your party's over. She loves a catered event like I do."

George gestured round at the party, which was now in full swing. "You kids are doing a wonderful job helping with this," she said.

Allie laughed. "Are you kidding?" she said, flicking her blond hair back over her shoulders. "This is fun! Tsk, tsk – unfolded napkin . . ." Zooming over to a nearby table, Allie did her wrist flick again and turned the napkin into another swan.

On the other side of the garden, George's daughter Jo was grumpily offering canapés, tugging at her bow-tie and looking miserable. Waiting on guests wasn't Jo's thing.

"Here," she said sourly, thrusting her tray under the nose of Renfro Xanx, a neat and rather dull little man in his thirties who ran the Falcongate stationery shop. "Eat that."

Renfro Xanx daintily chose and ate a single cheese straw. Somehow, he didn't spill any crumbs down his snow-white shirt. With a grunt, Jo stomped off to feed someone else.

"Well, not *all* of us think it's fun," Allie admitted, as Jo plodded past.

Over at the refreshment table, Max and Dylan's walnut-and-baguette cricket match was under way. Walnuts were flying in all directions. Dylan smacked one or two, and was now racing back and forth and yelling.

"And some of us make our *own* fun," Allie added.

To prove Allie's point, Dylan walloped a walnut across the garden. Timmy, Jo's dog, caught it triumphantly in a bread basket he was carrying in his mouth.

Silence fell as George tapped a glass with a spoon. *Ting ting ting.*

"Attention, Falcongate Rose Society," she said loudly, as Constable Stubblefield seized another handful of snacks. "It is time to unveil my prize roses!"

The members of the Falcongate Rose Society clapped as George opened her arms in the direction of a bed of vibrant pink roses.

"I give you – Pink Paradise!" George announced.

But somehow, the roses weren't pink any more.

As the applause faltered, the blooms turned brown and curled up. Little yellow bumps spread across the leaves and stems like a rash.

The guests murmured among themselves. Constable Stubblefield tucked one last pastry into her mouth, then bustled over to examine the plants.

"I'd call these roses rather more dead than usual," she declared.

"Something's wrong," George said anxiously, touching the dying flowers. "Roses don't get ill so quickly!"

Jo pushed through the crowd and hunkered down beside the plant. The yellow bumps had completely killed it. "Maybe they didn't *get* ill," she said thoughtfully. "Maybe someone *made* them ill . . ."

Chapter Two

The garden party broke up into small, worried groups. The conversation was the same everywhere. If this yellow blight had affected George's roses, whose roses would be next?

In the hubbub, the cousins glanced at each other. They knew the drill. They'd done stuff like this before. It was time to search for clues. There were *always* clues.

Sure enough, the first clue appeared after just a few minutes. After crawling through the greenhouse with her nose pressed to the soft earth, Jo pounced on something deep underneath one of the Pink Paradise rose bushes. She held up a crumpled cardboard tube.

"Look at this," she said, twisting it round so that everyone could see it. "The yellow powder on it looks a lot like the yellow powder on this rose." She dangled it between her fingers. "Exhibit A," she declared with a businesslike nod.

Over by the greenhouse workbench, Max had found something else.

"Look at these footprints," he said in excitement, pointing at a set of ridged prints in the earth. "They're huge! So that's Exhibit B, eh?"

Jo shook her head. "Let's make the roses Exhibit B," she suggested.

"And the footprints lead to the greenhouse door!" Allie exclaimed. "Exhibit Four!"

"Well, *three*," said Max, starting to look confused, "if we're switching from letters."

"Yes," Jo agreed. "The footprints were C once the roses were B—" She shook her head as if she had water in her ears. "You know what?" she said at last. "Let's just look for clues."

"Like this lock," said Dylan, over by the greenhouse door. "Jimmied open!"

The cousins rushed over to check out Dylan's

find. It was true. The door had been forced open. Someone had sabotaged Pink Paradise! But *who*? And why? Jealousy? Hatred of the colour pink?

The cousins watched as Falcongate's police officer made her way slowly through the greenhouse, glancing from side to side. There were still several canapé crumbs around her mouth.

"There's no lack of clues," Constable Stubblefield declared.

The cousins felt relieved. For once, it looked like Constable Stubblefield was up to the job of finding the villains!

"I'd be on to this like a bloodhound if it weren't for my spa massage appointment," continued the constable. She stretched. "I carry my tension in my upper buttocks," she added by way of explanation. "*Adieu*."

And Constable Stubblefield trotted off to her appointment.

Renfro Xanx, the stationer, pushed through the crowd. He pulled a spotless pair of gardening gloves from his pocket, and gingerly picked up a wilted rose. Jo thought about how dirty her mother got in the garden, and wondered how Renfro Xanx stayed so clean.

"My cousin Elihu is a chemist," Renfro Xanx told George, in a voice that was just as neat and clipped as he was. "Perhaps he can study this powder, and who knows . . . invent a cure?"

"I hope so," George said, absent-mindedly scratching a small, bumpy yellow rash on the back of her hand. She waved at her roses. "For the sake of Prudence . . . Penelope . . . Paulette . . ."

"Mum's got hundreds of roses," Jo told the others. "I bet we can solve this before she's done naming them all."

"Prunella . . . Peasie . . ." George continued dreamily as the cousins left the greenhouse and headed for the house. "Patricia . . . Pandora . . ."

"We should get a microscope and check out that powder on the tube," Max suggested to the others as they approached the porch of the main house. "And also look into why walnuts and baguettes are so perfect for cricket."

"Good idea!" Dylan said enthusiastically.

But before the boys could discuss edible cricket any further, an excitable African-American

10

girl ran out of the house towards them.

"Allie!" the girl squealed.

"Courtney!" Allie squealed back.

The two girls jumped into a complicated girlfriends kind of hug.

"Allie-Allie-Mal-ee-boo!" Courtney shrieked. "I am so excited to see you, I could explode!"

"I hope you don't," said Jo. "Clearing up the mess would be a nightmare."

"Oh!" said Allie, suddenly remembering her cousins. "Courtney, this is Jo, and my other cousins Dylan and Max. And this is Timmy."

Everyone murmured hellos. Timmy woofed politely.

Courtney nodded at them all. Then she rummaged through her bag and pulled out a magazine, which she waved under Allie's nose. "Look!" she said eagerly. "The latest issue of *Celeb Watch*! Huge pull out section on reality-show contestant hairstyles! Bizarre-o-tastic!"

"Great!" Allie patted her friend on the arm. "But I'll have to look at it later – we've stumbled on a mystery and we have to get right on to it . . ."

"Oh . . ." said Courtney. She looked deflated as

Allie turned away from her and went inside the house with the others.

With nothing better to do, Courtney followed.

Chapter Three

Courtney hovered by the fireplace as the Kirrin cousins gathered around the desk in George's study. Dylan flipped open his laptop. The others studied the tube.

"Looks torn in half," said Jo with a frown. "Like it's a postal tube and the addresses were torn off."

Allie looked more closely. "I can make out a few half-words . . ." she said after a minute. "*San*— and *Nor*—"

"*Santa Claus, North Pole!*" Max gasped, coming to life. "It's a wish list!"

"While Max pursues *that* theory . . ." Dylan said, typing busily at his laptop, "I'll try getting a complete list of English county names . . ."

Allie put the tube down on a table. She joined the others as they leaned in to watch Dylan's laptop screen.

"Allie-gal, it's mucho freezing," said Courtney. It was a chilly day for the time of year, and Courtney was shivering even though she was beside the fire. "Like that time we went skiing, remember? Sooo fun-tastic. We should do it again."

"Yeah, we will sometime," Allie replied absently.

"Good," Courtney nodded. She shivered again. "Still cold, though. Erm – is it OK to burn those old catalogues and newspapers and stuff?"

The others weren't listening. Courtney shrugged and scooped up the scattered papers beside Dylan's laptop.

"Woof!" Timmy barked suddenly as Courtney tossed an armful of papers on to the fire.

"Wait!" Jo gasped, realising what Courtney was doing. "You've got the tube!"

It was too late. The tube had caught fire and was already burning merrily.

"Ahh, I'm sorry – I didn't realise I had it!" Courtney clapped her hands to her face and looked appalled. "Oh, I'm such a dumbazoid, I could just faint!"

"It's OK, Court," Allie soothed.

"I am so accident-prone," Courtney groaned. "I actually sat on fly-paper once. Oh, and I caused my parents' garage to slide off a hillside."

Max looked impressed. "Oh, don't feel bad," he assured Courtney. "Accidents happen, believe *me*."

Gesturing wildly towards himself to prove the point, he managed to knock over a paperweight on the desk. The paperweight teetered, then fell off the desk and on to the foot-pedal of the study waste-paper bin. Some books stacked on top of the bin pinged across the room, flying straight into a shelf of ornaments, which collapsed in spectacular fashion. There was a moment of stunned silence.

"See?" Max panted. He rubbed his head, where it had been caught by a small vase. "But we can still study the footprints."

"Yes," Dylan agreed. "It must be impossible to throw a footprint into the fire."

Out in the greenhouse again, the large footprints were still in place. The kids followed them out of

15

the greenhouse and through some bushes with mounting excitement.

"These footprints are awesomely large," Allie gasped, placing one of her dainty feet beside the prints.

"Whoever did this must spend a fortune on huge shoes," Dylan said. He looked thoughtful. Whipping a tiny digital recorder from his pocket, he flipped it to *record*. "Note to self," he murmured, "open franchise selling huge shoes."

"You know," Jo said, "Constable Stubblefield has really big feet . . ."

This was an interesting theory. Could Constable Stubblefield really have done this to George's prize roses? Everyone peered more closely at the footprints.

"Stubblefield's not our man," Allie announced at last. "These are from some gross work boot. Stubblefield wears black pumps that were in style last never."

"We should take an imprint of these footprints," Max suggested.

Courtney was still hovering behind the sleuthing cousins. She sighed, and leaned back against the tall

garden-hose spout. The hose went wild, spraying everywhere. Timmy leaped for it, seizing it in his mouth as the others yelled with shock.

"Oh no!" Courtney gasped, turning crimson. "I . . . I must have leaned against the tap . . . !"

She rushed to turn off the water as Timmy fought on for control of the hose. But the damage was done.

"Well, you can't throw a footprint in the fire," Dylan said, staring sadly at the muddy mess at their feet. "But you can wash it away."

"Oooh . . . I could just crawl into a hole," Courtney moaned. "Now you're out of clues." She brightened for a moment. "You're as clueless as me!"

"Not quite," said Jo, keeping her temper with difficulty as Courtney giggled. She held up a soggy stub of paper. "This cinema ticket stub was squashed into the footprint. It must have belonged to the culprit."

"We should talk to the cinema owner," Max said as Courtney stopped giggling. He tried – and failed – to wring out his wet clothes without actually taking them off. "Plus we can use their high-powered hand dryer in the loo," he added, giving up.

The search for the villain who'd wrecked George's roses wasn't over yet. Everyone high-fived each other with relief. Everyone except – Jo noticed with interest – Courtney.

Chapter Four

The Falcongate cinema was a grand building on Falcongate High Street. It looked as if it had been designed for Hollywood, rather than the small, sleepy market town where it had ended up. The building towered over its neighbours, posters trumpeting the latest releases and music pouring through its great glass doors. All it needed was a plush red carpet across its wide steps, a gaggle of photographers and a queue of limousines to complete the look.

In Falcongate, none of these things was likely.

The Five, plus Courtney, took the steps up to the plush red lobby two at a time. They didn't have time to appreciate the architecture. They needed answers – and fast.

The cinema's owner, Mr Bicky, stood at the ticket office. He was eyeing everyone in the cinema lobby, daring someone – anyone – to misbehave. While the Five headed towards him, Courtney loitered beside an enormous display of an ancient Egyptian town square.

Jo cleared her throat. "Mr Bicky," she began politely. "We were wondering if—"

Mr Bicky held up his hand. "Pardon me one moment," he said. "NO RUNNING IN MY LOBBY!"

The Five almost leaped out of their skins. Mr Bicky whipped out a digital camera and snapped a picture of the man dashing past the ticket desk.

"I tolerate nothing but cinema-going perfection," said Mr Bicky, pocketing his camera again and turning back to the Kirrins. "If I spy a litterer or a gum-chewer, I take a photo, then ban the perpetrator for life."

Looking bored, Courtney prodded a display obelisk and yawned.

"We were wondering if you've noticed any

big-footed customers lately?" Jo persisted.

Mr Bicky nodded at once. "Yes, I banished a short, large-footed philistine whose mobile phone went off during the noon performance of *Exodus 2: The Pharaoh's Revenge.*"

"Is that what this is?" Courtney asked, her hand hovering over a cardboard Pharoah. "How mummy-riffic! It's just like Las Vegas." She frowned. "And, I guess, Egypt."

"I can't get his ring-tone out of my head," Mr Bicky continued. He started humming a tune. It was the Can-Can. "La-la, da-da-da-daa-daa, la-da-da-da-daa-daa . . ."

Max couldn't resist joining in. "Da-da-da-da . . ." he added obligingly as Mr Bicky tapped the rhythm out on the counter.

"Daa-daa, da-da . . . Hey!"

Now it was Courtney's turn. Singing merrily, she did a high Can-Can kick, caught the obelisk and sent it flying.

"Ahhh!" Courtney squealed in horror.

The obelisk knocked over several Pharaoh statues, which dominoed into a Sphinx. With a smashing sound, the Sphinx's nose broke off. The

Kirrin cousins gaped at the destruction. It had happened in a matter of seconds.

"Ohh, now I'm the clumsiest girl in ancient Egypt!" Courtney wailed. "Or Vegas. I could just crawl into a mummy case!"

At first, Mr Bicky was too stunned to react. Then, jerkily, he pulled his camera out and fired several shots in Courtney's direction. "Banned!" he roared, going purple. "Banned, I say!"

"You didn't happen to take a picture of the Can-Can man, did you?" Dylan enquired. Courtney skulked over to the door, looking sheepish.

Breathing heavily, Mr Bicky lowered his camera. "If my battery lasts, I can show you," he said, sounding a little calmer. He hit a button and started scrolling through his photos. "Gum-on-the-seat man, laser-pointer man . . . ah, here we are. Mobile phone-ringer desperado."

What a break! The Five looked at each other happily.

"Would it be OK if we borrowed your camera so I could download that picture on to my computer?" Dylan asked.

Mr Bicky handed over his camera. "Yes – I can

use my spare in the meantime," he said. "We've got a rugby club coming in tomorrow. I'll be snapping photos and taking names . . ." He glared once again at Courtney, who skulked a little closer to the doors.

Filled with excitement, the cousins left the cinema. The camera should give them some crucial information about the person who had done this to George's roses.

"Hey, this camera's exactly like mine, only I don't have that tacky strap!" Courtney exclaimed, seizing the camera from Dylan as he went to put it in his pocket. "Who needs that?"

Before anyone could stop her, she started removing the wrist strap – and tripped over a bump in the pavement.

"Whoah!"

The camera went flying into the air, landing in the back of a passing lorry filled with what looked like old junk.

"Wow," Courtney panted as the lorry whizzed on down the street and swerved round the corner, disappearing from view. "King-sized whoops!"

"That's Junkyard Jerome's lorry," Jo said. She

broke into a run. "If we don't beat him to the dump, we'll never get the camera back!"

"We'll take a short cut down Benjamin Hill," said Max, as everyone else took off after Jo. "Come on . . ."

Diving ahead of Jo, Max swerved into a nearby grocer's shop, which had a stack of empty apple boxes outside its doors.

"Could we borrow those empty fruit boxes?" Max asked quickly.

"Of course," said the grocer in surprise. "I was just about to send them to the dump."

Max grinned and seized a box. "Perfect!" he said, leaping in.

"Whoah, ungh . . ."

Allie and Courtney hopped into two more boxes, followed by Jo, Dylan and Timmy. And they tobogganed off down the road like a crazy bobsled team.

Chapter Five

Benjamin Hill was a wooded, bushy slope leading out of Falcongate towards the dump. It wasn't designed for apple-box tobogganing. But this didn't stop the Five. Not one bit.

Max zipped along ahead of the others, steering his box as best he could through the shrubs, twigs and trees that loomed up in all directions. The shouts and yells of the others told him that they weren't far behind. He trail-blazed the craggy, tree-lined slope, ripping through the undergrowth. Hitting a tree-root, he launched into the air like a box-shaped rocket. The rest followed at speed. They landed hard, but kept flying downwards.

"Go left!" Max roared. "Huge squirrel!"

Everyone swerved.

"Woahhhhh!"

The huge squirrel looked surprised. It fled up a tree that creaked under its weight.

More shrubs, bushes, rocks . . . and then they were tobogganing right into the dump itself, past old mattresses and rusty kitchen appliances. The apple boxes came to rest in a stinking pit of rotting fish and fruit. Timmy sniffed the air and pulled a face.

Moments later, Junkyard Jerome's lorry bumped, shook and swung into the dump.

"Hey, Mr Jerome!" Jo panted, struggling out of her apple box and rushing over to the truck.

Mr Jerome looked alarmed as Jo took a flying leap into the truck, landing with a bump.

"You've got our camera . . . !" she yelled in explanation.

Mr Bicky's camera had had a soft landing in the middle of a discarded old armchair. Jo triumphantly pulled it free. They still had the pictures!

Back at the house, George was bustling in the

kitchen. She heard Jo's voice out in the hall.

"Hi, Mum – we're home!"

"I'm in the kitchen, making eggs!" George called back, taking the egg boxes out of the fridge. As she put the eggs down on the counter, she frowned at the bumpy yellow rash on the backs of her hands. It had now spread to her arms and neck.

"Odd," George said in surprise, staring at the rash. "Yellow bumps. They look just like my poor roses."

She reached for an egg and made to crack it. Her arm twitched strangely, and she dropped the egg on the floor. Trying again, she cracked a second egg. This one joined the first.

"Hmm . . ." George said, suddenly feeling shaky as her legs started wobbling. "Very odd indeed."

Bang. Crash. Thump. Wobbling all over the place now, George bashed into pans, cutlery and crockery. Everything was smashing to the ground. A bottle of fizzy drink fell over and popped its lid, spraying sticky ooze over the entire mess.

"Woaah – woaah – wooaahhh," George muttered helplessly. What was wrong with her?

* * *

"Sounds like your mum's practising her juggling again," Max told Jo, cocking his head in the direction of the kitchen chaos as the cousins and Courtney headed into the study.

Dylan connected a cable to the back of his computer and settled down at the desk. "Camera's powered up," he said, checking Mr Binky's camera. "I just need to connect this cable—"

"Oh!" Courtney piped up, grabbing the camera from Dylan and pressing a few buttons. "I forgot to show you the most neat-rageous thing on this camera! When you press this button, it . . ." She paused, looking surprised. ". . . *'delete all'*?"

Dylan snatched back the camera. The screen was blank.

All that apple-box tobogganing to the stinky dump had been for nothing. With yet another demonstration of how accident-prone she was, Courtney had wiped the camera's memory clean.

"If you're so embarrassed you could crawl into a hole," said Jo drily as Courtney opened her mouth to apologise, "now would be a good time."

Back in the kitchen, George had made a spectacular

29

mess. Bowls and cups lay everywhere, smashed and broken on the floor and work surfaces. Somehow she'd managed to cook the eggs, but was now using the wrong end of the fork to eat them.

"Perhaps a good lie-down's in order," George said shakily to herself. Her legs were still very rubbery. She wobbled towards the door. Her speech was getting wobbly too, now. "Yes, a good bly-frown . . ." she mumbled. Her lips weren't cooperating. "Fligh gibble dibble flampjamp. Hmmm . . ."

Chapter Six

The next day, the cousins plus Timmy and Courtney left the cinema, looking very gloomy. Not even its fabulous display of *Exodus 2: The Pharoah's Revenge* posters could lift their spirits.

"So, banned for six weeks because we erased his photos," Max sighed. "I suppose we'll have to read books or something . . ."

A couple of teenagers in matching ensembles pushed past them on the cinema steps. It was Blaine and Daine Dunston, Falcongate's very own Gruesome Twosome.

"Out of our way, Kirrins," said Blaine. He was looking far too pleased with himself. "Renfro Xanx's cousin came up with a cure for Yellow Bumpy Rose Blight."

Blaine's twin sister Daine smirked. "Everyone's roses in Falcongate have the blight," she said.

"We're on our way to buy the cure," Blaine boasted. "So, to recap – out of our way."

Noses in the air, the Dunstons headed on up the pavement. The Kirrins glanced at each other, and followed the Dunstons along the road and into Renfro Xanx's stationery shop.

Blaine whipped round at the sound of the tinkling bell on the shop door. He scowled at the sight of Jo and the others. Jo gave him a tiny wave, which made him scowl even more.

"We're first," Daine said. "Ha!"

The Five noticed that Daine was scratching a bumpy yellow rash that was developing on the back of her hand. It reminded them of the rose blight.

Allie leaned in to examine the unsightly rash. "Love what you've done to your skin," she murmured.

Daine tucked her hands under her armpits. "It's a rub-on tattoo," she said defensively. "All the cool people in London have them."

There was a clattering noise from the back of the shop. Blaine and Daine swung round, looking expectant. Everyone saw an enormous bucket staggering in. Behind the bucket, they spotted the top of Renfro Xanx's carefully combed head.

Renfro Xanx set the bucket down and wiped his hands. He smoothed his already smooth hair. He didn't pay any attention to the Dunstons or the Kirrins.

Blaine leaned over the counter. "So, Mr Xanx, that's the cure?" he said eagerly, trying to peer inside the bucket.

Renfro Xanx gazed at Blaine. He gave a twitch of a smile. "Mix a cup of the powder with three cups of water, spray it on the roses and it fixes them right up," he said.

"Amazing," Jo said, impressed.

"Expensive – but well worth it," Renfro Xanx said.

"Great," said Blaine at once. He drummed his fingers impatiently on the counter. We'll take all of it. Who cares if it's expensive? We're rich."

"We'll be the only ones in town with healthy roses!" Daine said smugly as Renfro Xanx took the money from Blaine, smoothed it out, folded it neatly and tucked it into his pocket. "We'll win this year's Rose Fête for sure! And we'll *still* be rich."

The twins gave a spooky double smirk, turned on their well-shod heels and marched out of the shop, taking Renfro Xanx's entire stock of Yellow Bumpy Rose Blight cure with them.

"When is someone going to come up with a cure for the Dunstons?" Jo asked crossly.

Having nothing else to do, the kids headed for the Falcongate police station, to test for fingerprints on the cinema ticket stub Jo had found in the enormous footprint.

But when the Kirrins, Timmy and Courtney entered, the place was deserted.

Allie threw up her hands. "Shoot," she said. "Where's Constable Stubblefield when you need her?"

Dylan checked off a list on his fingers. "At lunch. At the romance-novel convention. At the spa. On holiday." He raised his eyebrows at the others. "Shall I go on?"

"No need," Jo said. "We can use her fingerprint

kit and test the ticket stub ourselves."

"Good idea," said Max as Jo pulled out the ticket stub and laid it on the desk. "The fingerprint kit is around here somewhere."

The Five started rummaging through Constable Stubblefield's desk and shelves. Timmy sniffed hard in all the corners, not wanting to be left out. Watching from the door, Courtney hunched her shoulders and stuck her hands in her pockets. All this sleuthing was starting to get her down.

Jo had moved across Constable Stubblefield's office to where the constable's Medal for Bravery (picked up at a local jumble sale and one of Constable Stubblefield's proudest possessions) twinkled on the wall. Reflected in the shimmery gold metal, Jo saw Courtney move towards the desk and slip something in her pocket.

Courtney headed over to the prison cell in the corner of the station.

"Wow," she murmured, peering into the cell. "I've never seen a jail cell before." She sniffed and pulled a face. "Ewww – it smells like my brother's room! Mucho gross-ful. Needs some air."

"Found it!" Max said triumphantly, producing the

fingerprinting kit and waving it in the air as Courtney flung open the station door and took a couple of lungfuls of fresh air. "Now let's check for prints."

Dylan turned to the desk. His eyes widened. "Where did the ticket stub go?" he wailed, hunting through the scattered papers and sweetie wrappers. "Oh, another missing clue! I'm embarrassed for us, really I am."

"Oh, no!" Courtney gasped. "It must have blown out the door after I opened it!" She clapped a hand to her forehead. "Oh, I feel so bad, I could just die!"

"Well, I'm here to save your life," Jo said, staring at Courtney very hard. "Empty your pockets."

Allie looked shocked. "Jo!" she said crossly. "Courtney's my friend. She wouldn't do anything!"

Jo kept looking at Courtney. Turning as red as one of George's roses, Courtney felt in her pocket and pulled out the ticket stub.

"I *knew* you'd taken it," Jo said, snatching the stub. She turned to the others. "She's been interfering with our clues on purpose!"

Max lifted a finger and pointed it at Courtney. "So *you* poisoned the roses!" he said dramatically.

"Before you even arrived from America!" Then, realising that his theory made no sense, he lowered his finger sheepishly. "I withdraw the accusation!" he muttered. "You're free to go."

Allie was trying to understand what had just happened. "Courtney," she began, struggling for words. "Why would you be so . . ."

"Lame-rageous?" offered Dylan.

"You spend all your free time here, away from me," Courtney confessed, twisting her trainer into the carpet. "You're always, like . . ." She made little quote marks in the air with her fingers: ". . . 'solving mysteries'. I thought if you couldn't solve this one, you'd stay home more."

Allie looked surprised. "I don't come here to solve mysteries!" she said. "I come here to spend time with my cousins."

"I'm touched," Max said, looking pleased.

"I guess I kind of left you out of things, Courtney," Allie admitted, thinking things through. Her friend had come all the way from LA, and Allie had hardly spoken to her. "I should have made you part of our team."

"Thanks," Courtney said with a wobbly smile.

"That sounds great." She smiled a little wider. "Great-tastic!"

Allie gave her friend another one of her special girlfriend hugs. Courtney hugged her right back. Jo sighed. She had a feeling this would go badly wrong, but there was nothing for it.

"OK – she's on the team," she said. "Get her a jumper and let's get on with this."

Courtney looked delighted. She flung her arms around Jo. Jo pushed her off.

"Eeeww . . . oh . . ." said Courtney, disappointed.

Jo pointed at her. "And don't do that," she warned.

Chapter Seven

Everyone turned as Constable Stubblefield came into the police station. She looked odd, even by Constable Stubblefield's standards. Wearing a spa robe and some fluffy slippers, she was wobbling from side to side as if she was about to fall over.

"Hello, all," said the police officer cheerfully. She grabbed hold of the edge of her desk just as her knees gave way. "My spa treatment overran. Turns out, if you don't tell them to stop, they don't."

Dylan stared at the constable, who was now sinking to the floor. "Must have been some massage," he said with a whistle. "You look *really* relaxed."

Constable Stubblefield smiled rather foolishly. "Best massage of nnnyyy mmmyffeee," she mumbled.

Allie frowned. "Come again?" she said, puzzled.

The police officer raised her hand to scratch at something on her neck.

"Hey," Jo gasped, starting forward. "That's the same yellow rash I saw on Blaine and Daine."

"And on the roses," Max put in.

Dylan raised a finger. "I'll tell you what it is," he announced. "The Yellow Bumpy Rose Blight."

Constable Stubblefield twitched and giggled down on the floor.

"Right . . ." Allie said, thinking hard. "Both the Dunstons and Constable Stubblefield touched Aunt George's roses. So the virus . . ."

Max punched the air. "Has mutated to infect humans," he said in triumph. "Bam! Take that, mystery!"

"We need to check on Mum and see if she's got the virus, too," said Jo, sounding worried. Digging in her pocket for her mobile, she punched in her home number.

"Dad?" she said, when Ravi answered. "I haven't seen Mum since this morning – is she acting funny in any way?"

Back at the house, Ravi glanced out of the kitchen window. George was trying to water the plants. Her wobbly arms and legs weren't making it easy It looked more like the hose was watering *her*.

"Flibbadee, flobbadee, flabadedee . . ." George giggled, getting a faceful of water for her trouble.

"Funny as in 'Oh, you made a joke'?" Ravi said into the phone. "Or funny as in 'She's waltzing with a garden hose'?"

41

Jo covered the receiver with her hand. "We have an epidemic here," she told the others in a grim voice. She spoke into the phone again. "Keep a close eye on Mum," she told her dad. "I'll call back later."

There was a rush of bicycle wheels outside the police station. The Five ran to the window, to see Blaine and Daine Dunston whizzing past. They were wobbling all over the place.

"Yumpo!!!" mumbled Blaine. "Gooby-nup!!!"

"If they're infected like Stubblefield and Aunt George, then they're a disaster-balloon waiting to pop," said Dylan, watching as the Dunstons and their bikes flew on down the road.

Everyone ran for the door, leaving Constable Stubblefield mumbling happily somewhere underneath her desk. Max jumped on his skateboard. The others grabbed their bikes. With Timmy barking like mad, they chased after the Dunstons. The twins were out of control!

"Woahhhhh!"

The bucket of Yellow Bumpy Rose Blight cure was in Daine's bicycle basket and it wobbled from side to side as the Dunstons crashed through a

"Do Not Enter" sign in front of a building site. As Blaine and Daine raced off in two different directions, the Kirrins, Timmy and Courtney split up. They were determined not to let the Dunstons out of their sight.

Blaine was heading wildly on to a narrow plank which lay across a deep hole in the ground. The board was nearly as wobbly as Blaine. But Blaine didn't seem to care. His eyes were closed, and he was whooping happily.

Max hunkered down on his skateboard. He picked up speed. He raced on to the plank – just as Blaine left the other end. The plank teetered and tipped upwards.

"Impromptu ramp . . . sweet!" Max grinned.

He launched into the air, high above Blaine. As he landed, he threw himself at Blaine and yanked him off his bike. They both ended up in a muddy puddle.

"Woaaah!"

"Heyyyyy . . ."

"Oooff!!"

Meanwhile, Allie and Dylan were following Daine up a ramp towards the first floor of the newly constructed building. Daine's bike whizzed along a loadbearing steel beam. There was nothing at the other end of the beam but open air!

Sprinting ahead of Dylan, Allie reached the near end of the beam just in time to angle it towards the ground. Halfway along, Daine now found herself pedalling downhill, picking up speed as she went.

"Wooahhhhhh!" she squealed.

"Come on, Timmy!" Jo yelled.

Bending down low over her handlebars, Jo raced for a nearby concrete-mixer. With Timmy's help, she upended the mixer and poured out a mini-lake of concrete. It wasn't a moment too soon. Daine slid down the beam and into the concrete puddle, where her bike wheels stopped dead.

"Aargghhh!"

The sudden halt flung the bucket of Bumpy Yellow Rose Blight cure into the air. Its lid flew off, and the powder spilt into an open cauldron of hot roofing tar. It was completely ruined.

"Don't tell me that was the only blight cure left," Dylan panted, climbing off his bike.

"Shloooov. Muhp-meem . . ." Daine mumbled, and collapsed sideways.

"I think that was an affirmative," said Max.

They all stared at the remains of the blight cure. Queen of the understatement, Allie clapped her hand to her forehead and summed it up.

"Uh-oh . . ."

Chapter Eight

Only one person knew how to get hold of more Yellow Bumpy Rose Blight cure. Which was how the Five plus Courtney found themselves back at Renfro Xanx's stationery shop in Falcongate half an hour later.

"Mr Xanx, is that cure powder only for flowers?" Jo asked, leaning over the counter. "Because the Yellow Bumpy Rose Blight is infecting *people*, too."

Renfro Xanx's pale face turned paler. "What?!" he gasped. "It's not supposed to—" He stopped, looking flustered. "I mean, my cousin's making some more – you can ask him if it would work for people."

A man none of the Five had ever seen before now came into the shop. He looked just like Renfro, only stockier. He stared suspiciously at them.

"Are you Mr Xanx's cousin?" said Allie hopefully. "We really need another batch of cure powder—"

As she spoke, Elihu Xanx's mobile went off.

La-la, da-da-da-da daa-daa, la-da-da-da daa-daa . . .

The tune was familiar. Automatically, Max started humming along. "Da-da-da-da-da, la la la la la la da . . . D'ah . . ." He dried up, realising.

It was the Can-Can.

The cousins exchanged looks. Elihu Xanx was the *cinema* guy?

"Well, great . . ." Dylan told Renfro Xanx into the awkward silence. They needed to buy some time. "Uh, let us know when you have that cure powder ready."

The cousins backed out of the shop. The Xanx cousins watched them silently.

Outside the shop, the Five and Courtney gathered together.

"He must be the big shoe guy from the cinema," Dylan hissed. "*He* put the powder on the roses!"

47

They had to listen to what the Xanxes were planning! Running round to the back of the shop, they checked the door and windows. Everything was closed. Max knelt down and peered through the keyhole on the back door. "Attempting visual confirmation . . ." he said, resting his cheek against the door. ". . . but nothing." He got to his feet. "The key's in the keyhole on the other side."

"We need to find out what they're talking about in there," Allie insisted.

Allie's phone started ringing cheerfully. Allie pounced on it and clicked it on. "Hello?"

"Hi best friend!" Courtney giggled into her phone, standing about two feet behind Allie. "I just had the most amazingly amazing idea! Who's got some string?"

Allie sounded doubtful. "I've got bubblegum-flavoured dental floss . . ."

She pulled the floss from her pocket and handed it over. Courtney took a long piece. Then she tied it round Allie's phone, which was still connected.

"Brilliant," Dylan breathed, staring at Courtney's

invention. "We just lower it into the shop and we stay tuned."

Jo took Allie's phone and shimmied up to the shop roof like a cat. She carefully lowered the phone on its thin pink string, straight down the chimney and into the shop.

Max smiled broadly. "Put that sucker on speakerphone," he said.

Courtney hit the speakerphone button on her phone. Everyone listened in.

Renfro Xanx was speaking.

". . . our rose virus is spreading to people!"

"It must have mutated ..." Elihu's voice was lower than his cousin's. "Hey – we'll make twice as much money! I'll come up with a cure for people, and we can sell two antidotes! Cha-ching!"

The Five looked at each other. Jo gave a thumbs-up. Bingo!

Elihu was still talking.

"We stick with our plan to crop-dust blight powder all over the countryside. The plane's waiting, we've got three gallons of powder – we're set."

Courtney almost dropped the phone. There

would be a wobble epidemic!

"We've got to stop them!" Dylan said urgently. "We need to get inside . . . we need to distract them!"

Thinking on her feet, Allie grabbed Jo and Courtney and dragged them round to the front of the shop. She knocked hard. After a minute, Renfro and Elihu opened the door.

"Hi," said Allie desperately. "Um . . . *We wish you a Merry Christmas, we wish you a Merry Christmas. We wish you a Merry Christmas . . .*"

Jo and Courtney joined in.

"*And a Happy New Year!*"

"Woof," added Timmy.

The Xanx cousins looked confused.

"See er," Allie improvised, "my friend isn't going to be here at Christmas, so this is my chance to sing with her. *Good King Wenceslas looked out, on the Feast of Stephen . . .*"

At the back of the shop, Operation Keyhole was well under way. Max had found a sheet of newspaper which he slid under the door, while Dylan wiggled a straightened paperclip into the keyhole. There was a *plop* as the key landed on the newspaper inside. Very carefully, Max slid the newspaper back out. The key glittered at them.

"Easy-peasy," said Max, picking up the key and winking at Dylan.

Chapter Nine

Very quietly, Max and Dylan let themselves into the back of the stationery shop. They could still hear Allie and the others desperately singing their way through a collection of Christmas carols. They didn't have long before the Xanx cousins returned. Most people got bored after a maximum of three Christmas carols – and that was at Christmas-time.

"What are we looking for?" Max whispered as they poked about in the store room.

"Their blight powder," Dylan hissed back. He moved a couple of boxes and hunted through the shelves. "If they dust the crops with it, Falcongate will become Yellowbumpygate."

"Then I suppose it's a good job I've found it," Max said, straightening up with a large bucket of blight powder in his arms.

"Perfect," Dylan grinned. "I'll bet our local doctor can make an antidote from analysing this powder."

"That doctor can do anything," said Max optimistically. "Remember my broken arm? Totally not broken any more. Look . . ."

Tucking the bucket of blight powder under his arm, he swung the other arm in circles. "Feels great," he said, still swinging. "I can swing it all day, if I want to. Some days, I do."

Bang.

"Oww!"

Max rubbed his arm where it had whacked into a large box. A huge stream of ball-point pens clattered out of the box and plinked loudly into a set of scales.

Out in front, the girls had run out of carols and had moved on to folk songs. Renfro and Elihu were still listening politely, but Elihu was starting to sneak glances at his watch. How much longer were they going to make this diversion last?

"Parsley, sage, rosemary and thyme . . ." the girls sang on.

The sound of clattering pens reached the Xanxes. Spinning round, they both ran back into the shop.

"Is this yours?" Max asked politely, holding up the powder as Renfro and Elihu skidded to a halt at the door to the store cupboard. "Or is it for anybody?"

Renfro Xanx's normally mild expression twisted into a snarl. He pulled on a nearby lever. An avalanche of polystyrene packing pellets rained down on to Max from a chute above.

"Heyyyy!" Max yelled, temporarily blinded.

"Thank you," snapped Renfro, snatching the bucket out of Max's flailing hands. He ran from the shop, his cousin close behind.

"What happened?" Jo panted, rushing into the store cupboard with the others.

Dylan dusted polystyrene pellets off his shoulders. "They took the powder and took their leave," he said gloomily.

"So we have to take off," Max added, "before *they* take off."

* * *

Half an hour later, Renfro and Elihu Xanx were revving up the engines on a small two-seater monoplane with an open cockpit. They started taxiing out on to a small, flat field they were using as a runway, waggling their tail fin and preparing to take flight.

The Kirrins, Timmy and Courtney squealed through the apple orchard that stood beside the field, on an assortment of bikes, skateboards and

furry feet. They raced on to the runway. But the plane was already too far ahead, bumping along the ground.

A small garden shed stood at the side of the field. But since when did garden sheds have bristling antennae springing from their roofs like crazy hairdos?

Dylan was the first inside the shed. He examined a small radio that lay on the wooden workbench and flipped a switch. Leaning down to the microphone, he started speaking in an extra deep voice.

"Flight zero-zero-one, control here . . . please turn right, westbound."

Up in the plane, Elihu and Renfro Xanx automatically obeyed the instructions they could hear through their headsets.

"Good," Dylan continued deeply. "Continue to turn and proceed to the control tower . . . well, it's more of a shed, actually . . ."

Elihu obediently turned back and headed for the shed.

"What's going on?!" Renfro shouted to his cousin across the din of the plane. "According to my map, this isn't the right way!"

Elihu's eyes widened as he caught sight of the Five and Courtney staring at him through the grimy shed windows. "Boy, those kids won't give up!" he snarled.

"Boy, those guys won't give up!" Max said, unwittingly echoing Elihu Xanx as the little plane swung away again and headed back up the runway.

He ran outside the shed, hopped up on to the tin roof and yanked off a boomerang-shaped antenna. Then he hefted the boomerang just as the plane was about to leave the ground.

The boomerang antenna sliced through the monoplane's rudder like a hot knife through butter. It then flew back to Max, who caught it and reattached it to the shed roof.

The plane was out of control. Elihu and Renfro fought to control the wildly swinging aircraft. But it plunged off the field and straight into the next-door apple orchard, slicing through the apples with its whirling propeller.

Snap! Snap! The wings were ripped off by trees as the plane careered on through the orchard. Apples bounced on the fusilage. Apple sauce rained down on the Xanxes like sweet sludge. Coughing and choking, the conniving cousins struggled out of the plane and tried to make a run for it. Jo was waiting for them beside a large water tank.

"Right this way, gentlemen," she said cheerfully, and turned on the pressure hose.

Renfro and Elihu were knocked off their feet by the explosion of water. As Courtney and Allie arrived to pull a pair of bright orange windsocks over the villains, Max, Dylan and Timmy joined them, triumphantly holding the intact bucket of blight powder high in the air.

"Heyyyy!" moaned Renfro.

"Owwwww!" groaned Elihu.

"Wow," Courtney gushed. "Now I get why you guys love solving crimes so much." She scooped up a cup of fresh apple sauce and took a taste. "Hmm," she said with a grin. "This fresh apple sauce is sauce-tabulously apple-dacious!"

Chapter Ten

The Falcongate Rose Society had gathered together in George's garden once again. George's roses were pink and blooming without a speck of yellow blight anywhere to be seen. George too was back to her old self – as were Constable Stubblefield and the Dunston twins.

Applause was ringing out across the lawn. But this time, the applause was for the Five and their new-found associate, Courtney.

"Well done, yet again, young Kirrins," said Constable Stubblefield cheerfully. She nodded at Courtney. "Plus a stranger whom I don't recognise."

Allie introduced her friend. "It's Courtney."

"Yes," said Jo wryly. "She made things more complicated than they needed to be, but in the end, she really was part of the team."

George had even more twigs in her hair than usual. "Well, thanks to the team, our local doctor came up with the cure for Yellow Bumpy Rose Blight," she said happily. "My little rose friends are all better now." She bent down to the nearest rose bush and tickled a couple of blooms under their petally chins. "Aren't you, my wittle-wosey-buddie-wuddies . . ."

Courtney frowned as George continued talking nonsense to her flowers. "Uh-oh – I don't think your aunt is completely cured," she said.

"Nah, that's just how she is," Allie grinned.

Max wandered over to the buffet table. His eyes lit up at the sight of the bowl of walnuts. Grabbing a couple, he started tossing them from hand to hand. "Baguette-and-walnut-cricket, anyone?" he said hopefully.

Dylan seized a baguette. "I think it's a splendid idea to play a rousing game of such elegance and class on this lovely day," he agreed, lining up the baguette in his best batting pose.

Max pitched the walnut to Dylan. As the little brown blur whizzed towards the baguette bat, Dylan swung with all his might. He smashed the walnut, sending it straight back to Max. Max ducked. The walnut ricocheted around the well-dressed Rose Society crowd, smashing a glass, pinging off Blaine's forehead and finally thwacking Stubblefield in the lower back.

"Oww!" groaned Blaine.

"Owww!" yelled Constable Stubblefield, leaping out of her skin. She landed hard, dropping her selection of canapés. "Well, that just undid all the beneficial work on my upper buttocks," she sighed, rubbing hard at her ample bottom. "Back to the spa go I."

Allie nudged her friend. "Courtney, we should do some relaxing, too. How 'bout a picnic at the beach?"

"OK," Courtney grinned. "The sandwiches and fruit salad are on me."

"Now you're talking," said Max happily.

Jo slung her arm round Courtney's shoulders. "Yes," she said, "you should visit more often . . ."

Epilogue

Jo peered through the viewfinder on Dylan's camera and panned around George's study until she came to rest on Allie.

"Sticky Situation Number Fourteen," she announced. "You Have To Listen Through A Wall."

Allie put on her best photo face – a kind of rictus grin. "You shouldn't eavesdrop, but sometimes you need to listen into another room, to find out what spies are doing, or what you're getting for your birthday," she told the camera. She held up a glass tumbler, which she placed against the wall. "You can hear through most walls with an ordinary drinking glass," she continued, adjusting the tumbler so that it was level with her ear. "It works like a doctor's stethoscope."

She listened. Jo waited patiently, zooming in and out on Allie's nose when she got bored.

"Hmm . . ." said Allie, cocking her head.

On the other side of the wall, Dylan was also listening through a tumbler.

A tumbler listening to a tumbler was never really going to work.

"I can't hear what they're doing in there," Dylan complained to Max, who was standing beside him. He took the tumbler off the wall and looked at it in disappointment. "This glass isn't working."

Back in the study, Allie carefully removed her tumbler and beckoned to Jo. Jo zoomed in a little closer.

"Sticky Situation Number Fifteen," Allie whispered, thumbing towards the wall. "Someone's listening to *you*."

Jo gave a wicked grin. "This one's easy . . ." she said.

Between them, Jo and Allie quickly produced a bass drum and a pair of cymbals. They crashed them smartly together, right up against the wall.

There was a crash on the far side of the wall as Dylan dropped his tumbler and covered both his ears.

"Wahhhhh!"

LOOK OUT FOR THE WHOLE SERIES!

THE CASE OF THE GUY WHO LOOKS
PRETTY GOOD FOR A 2000 YEAR-OLD

**Hodder
Children's
Books**

A division of Hachette Children's Books

Special thanks to Lucy Courtenay and Artful Doodlers

Copyright © 2009 Chorion Rights Limited, a Chorion company

First published in Great Britain in 2009 by Hodder Children's Books

3

A Catalogue record for this book is available from the British Library

ISBN 978 0 340 97086 7

Typeset in Weiss by Avon DataSet Ltd,
Bidford on Avon, Warwickshire

Printed and bound in Great Britain by
Clays Ltd, St Ives plc

The paper and board used in this paperback by Hodder Children's Books are natural recyclable products made from wood grown in sustainable forests. The manufacturing processes conform to the environmental regulations of the country of origin.

Hodder Children's Books
a division of Hachette Children's Books
338 Euston Road, London NW1 3BH
An Hachette Livre UK Company
www.hachettelivre.co.uk

Chapter One

The sun was sinking into the sea and the light was starting to fade as four sea kayaks paddled into view. The Famous Five followed the tree-lined shore, steering clear of swirling currents that splashed against the rocks. Some were finding this easier than others.

"I'm paddling the SEA in my little KAYAK," Allie sang lustily. She avoided a nasty bit of reef more by luck than anything. *"I'm happy as can BE, and . . ."* She stopped. Her paddle trailed to one side as she frowned, turning her kayak away from the shoreline.

Riding up ahead in Jo's kayak, Timmy looked

1

round at the silence. He wagged his tail enquiringly.

"Uh," said Allie, remembering to pull her paddle out before the kayak turned round completely, "nothing rhymes with kayak."

"Blackjack," Dylan offered from behind Allie. His glasses were spattered with sea water. "Old shack . . . haystack . . ."

Timmy barked sharply.

"Dog snack," Jo added.

Allie tossed her damp blond hair back over her shoulders and thought about this. She remembered to paddle again just before Dylan bumped into her.

"Strained . . . back . . ." Max wheezed.

Max's kayak was well behind the rest. Veins were popping in his forehead with the effort of pulling on his paddles. The kayak looked dangerously low in the water.

Jo shifted round to look back at her trailing cousin. "You wouldn't be struggling so hard if you hadn't tied a tree stump to your kayak," she said.

An enormous tree stump bobbed and swayed in the water behind Max.

2

"I also . . . loaded it . . . with bricks," Max panted proudly.

Allie frowned, almost steering into the rocks again. "I guess I'm not an experienced kayaker," she said. "I filled mine with drinking water and food supplies."

"I've entered . . . the Falcongate Junior Iron Man competition," Max panted. Reaching down into the kayak, he picked up a couple of bricks and hefted them into the water. "I'm in constant training," he said, raising his voice over the splash. "Becoming Super Max!"

For the benefit of his three cousins, he flexed his muscles. He stopped and examined his hand, looking worried. "Ow," he complained. "I've got a hangnail."

Up ahead, Jo tensed. "Hey," she said sharply. "What's that in the woods?"

She pointed towards the shore. The trees were almost in darkness now. But deep in the woods on the rocks above the water level, they all saw a bright orange glow. It pulsed strangely in the evening mist. Timmy growled. The cousins stopped paddling to get a better look. Now they could hear

3

a loud hissing sound as well.

"Ugh – I forget," Allie said in a high-pitched voice. "Do you still have dragons in England?" Since Allie was from America, it was a fair question.

Dylan swallowed. "Apparently," he said. "And I left all my dragon-fighting gear at home. What bad luck."

Jo's face set into the determined expression that her cousins both feared and admired. "Whatever that is, I want to find out more about it," she said. "Come on! Paddle!"

She turned her canoe and began paddling towards the shore. There was nothing for it. The others followed.

Well, most of them followed.

"Not . . . making . . . progress," Max groaned, struggling to move.

Sighing, Dylan turned back. Max's tree stump had got tangled with a buoy.

"Tree stump . . . caught . . . on buoy," Dylan teased as he unhooked his cousin.

Max felt his kayak move again. "That's better," he announced. "Stand back for Super Max!" With a burst of energy, he bent low and paddled in a blur

after the others. After a couple of minutes, he put his paddle down. "Great," he said, sounding annoyed as he examined his palms. "Now I'm getting a blister."

Chapter Two

The Five beached their kayaks and tied them up. Then they made their way up the rocky bluff. It was slow going. The mist was thickening, and it was growing darker. By the time they reached the place where they'd seen the flickering orange light, it was so foggy that no one could see a thing.

"I don't see the light anymore," said Dylan, from somewhere in the billowing greyness.

"I see something!" Allie shouted. "I'm walking towards it!"

Twigs crackled underfoot as Allie started blundering through the woods.

Then: "OOF!"

There was the sound of two people crashing into each other.

"Oof," Jo said, echoing Allie. "You walked towards my *forehead*."

Dylan was getting fed up. "Let's check in this clearing," he shouted, waving his arms just in case anyone could see him. "It looks empty, but at least there's less fog."

The cousins raced out of the foggy woods towards the clearing, narrowly missing several trees. Dylan had been right about the fog. It was lifting. However, day was still marching towards night. Things were certainly clearer – but also a whole lot darker.

The Five moved carefully across the clearing. Jo produced a torch. In the very centre of the clearing, they saw a large, uneven four-sided shape marked out on the ground. The grass around its edges was crushed and burnt.

"What could have made this?" said Allie, looking puzzled.

Dylan paced the four sides of the shape, studying it from all angles. "Hmm," he said at last. "It's trapezium shaped. The grass is singed around

the edges. My guess is a very heavy, hot trapezium."

Max knelt down near the imprint. He studied it carefully. The others watched, wondering if he'd found something.

Max straightened up, looking calm. "It's pretty obvious what this is," he said.

The others looked amazed. Max was the kind of guy whose brains were more often in his muscles than his head. And he'd worked it out *already*?

"Landing gear of an alien spaceship," Max continued with a shrug. "The engines fried the grass when it took off. Duh."

8

Jo felt quite relieved. It was reassuring to know Max was as weird as ever.

"And look at this," Max added, pouncing on a small chunk of leathery material that lay in the grass beside the imprint. "Tough, leathery alien skin. They shed their skin! They're like lizards!"

This was going *beyond* weird. Just as Jo wondered what she could say to Max that wouldn't hurt his feelings, Timmy trotted up with something in his mouth.

"No, wait," said Max, seeing what Timmy was carrying. He looked disappointed as he pulled a piece of plastic from Timmy's jaws. "It's not skin . . . it must be a piece of spicy salami. Timmy found the wrapper."

Jo took the strip of salami gingerly from Max. She tossed it to Timmy. "Good boy, Timmy," she said, grinning. "Have some alien skin."

As Timmy settled down to his treat, Jo felt around in her pockets for a camera. Jo was the kind of girl whose pockets never simply contained a ball of string and a box of matches. "We can take photos of this clearing and grab some samples of the grass," she said, finding her camera and snapping off

several shots. "Maybe that will help us work this out."

"And then let's get back to the beach and set up camp," said Allie, rubbing her arms. The evening air was getting cold. "We'll have dinner, some hot tea, and a lovely, lazy night."

The night was lazy. The morning was anything but.

PPPPEEEEEEPPPPP!

Jo and Allie jerked awake at the shrill sound of a police whistle blasting down the beach where they had set up camp. Rubbing their bleary eyes, Allie and Jo crawled out of their tent to see Constable Stubblefield, Falcongate's finest – well, only – police officer pacing the beach, her whistle clamped firmly between her lips.

Timmy stuck his nose out of his small dog tent and sniffed. A little further away, Dylan, who hadn't got round to putting his glasses on yet, tripped over his tent's guy ropes.

"Constable Stubblefield, do you know what time it is?" Jo said, as the others muttered and yawned.

Constable Stubblefield blew another sharp blast on her whistle. "It's six a.m. Greenwich Mean Time.

One a.m. Eastern Standard Time. Ten p.m. Pacific Standard Time," she announced, hitching up her trousers. "And in Australia, it's even later!" she added, just for effect.

Jo closed her mouth, which was hanging open. "She knows what time it is," she admitted.

Constable Stubblefield advanced on the cousins' tents. As she was a large person, it was an alarming sight. "This coastline is officially off-limits, from fifty degrees, thirty-six minutes north, to three degrees twenty-two minutes west," she continued.

Allie yawned. "She's strong on geography, too," she said.

Max came jogging into view. He'd clearly been on an early morning training session.

"Max," Dylan said, staring at his cousin's bulging tracksuit. "Is there someone else in your clothes with you, or did you put on twenty kilos overnight?"

Panting hard, Max held out the bottom of his shirt. A cascade of small rocks fell out.

Dylan clicked his fingers. "Oh, he was running with *rocks* in his clothes," he said, and rolled his eyes. "I should have guessed."

Max was jogging on the spot. Now he'd dropped the rocks, he was looking quite jaunty. "I don't like getting up early, but I need all the exercise I can get," he said chirpily, lifting his knees high. "Plan A is working the delts, the lats and the traps . . ." To demonstrate, he picked up one of the kayaks and lifted it above his head. He wobbled. "Ow – pebble in my shoe!" he shouted, hopping left and falling over. The kayak fell on top of him like a large and unflattering hat.

"Oofff – owwww," Max groaned.

Nothing that Max did ever surprised Dylan. "And Plan B seems to be falling on your bum," he observed.

Jo struggled to her feet and pulled her jacket round herself. "Constable Stubblefield," she said, "this is our favourite stretch of beach in the whole county. What's going on here?"

Constable Stubblefield opened her mouth to reply. But it was a man's voice that floated down the beach towards them all.

"I can answer that!"

Chapter Three

A balding, excitable-looking man came bouncing towards them. The thick, pebble-lensed glasses he was wearing made his eyes look enormous. Slung around his tummy was a tool belt. The belt bristled with so many picks, hammers and brushes that he jingled as he walked.

"What's going on here is science!" shouted the little man busily. "S-C-I-E-N-C-E! Archaeology! Paleoanthropology! The wonders of the ancient world!"

Allie pushed back her hair. "Looks like someone's had his morning coffee," she yawned.

"Not a hundred metres from here, I've made a

find," added the man rapidly. "Not a minor find. A *major* find."

Max gasped. "Atlantis!" he croaked. "You found *Atlantis!*"

"Well," replied the man after a moment. "Not *that* major."

"You didn't happen to find a purple scrunchy, did you?" said Allie, pushing back her hair again. "Because I lost one about a week ago."

The little man looked relieved at Allie's more realistic expectations. "This is somewhere *between* a scrunchy and a mythical lost continent," he said.

"If it's closing down this beach, it better be good," said Jo. She folded her arms. "What have you found?"

A little later that day, the Five discovered just what had been found. Down in the middle of Falcongate, the excitable Rupert Downpilt was gathering a number of spectators as he stood beside a large, draped object. The Five hopped off their bikes, straining to get a view over the crowd.

"Ladies and gentlemen," Rupert Downpilt began, twitching at the sheet covering the object. "I give

you – the Falcongate Mariner! A visitor from your ancient past!"

With a flourish, he pulled the sheet away from the object. The crowd gasped. A perspex case containing the leathery remains of a skeletal man stood before their eyes.

"Wow," Allie said, fascinated. "I've seen pictures, but never a real mummy. See what happens when you don't moisturise?"

"I can't see," Max complained, craning his neck to get a better view round the extremely tall person standing in front of him. "Guess I may as well work the old quads . . . and *jump!*"

He began leaping up and down like a frog, keeping it up for about five seconds before he slipped and fell over.

"There's Plan B again," Dylan sighed, polishing his glasses on his hoodie. "Falling on your bum."

Rupert Downpilt was still speaking.

"I believe the Mariner is a Bronze Age fisherman. Bronze Age!" He waved his arms exuberantly. Several people in the crowd stepped backwards. "There could be an entire fishing village buried along the coast!"

"So that's why the beach is closed down," Allie gasped, as a hubbub rippled through the spectators. "So he can find an ancient village *as old as time itself!*"

Dylan put his glasses back on. "Pretty impressive," he said. "Most days, I can't even find clean socks to wear."

Someone tall and elegant with an upturned nose and buck teeth had just stepped up to stand beside Rupert Downpilt. "Thank you, Rupert Downpilt,"

she twittered. The Five flinched at the odd, pig-like snort of laughter she added at the end of her sentence, as if Rupert Downpilt was an excellent joke. "Yes, my friends, I am County Councillor Rowena Pruitt. Please," she added, and snorted again as she held up her hand, "hold your applause."

Looking bored now, the audience shifted their feet and started checking their watches.

"Looks like that won't be a problem," Dylan murmured to the others.

"For the greater glory of Falcongate," Rowena Pruitt tittered on, "I decree the coastline off-limits for such time as Mr Downpilt requires. Hip-hip-hooray!"

Rowena Pruitt gave another snorty giggle, and posed pompously beside the Falcongate Mariner for a photographer to take her picture.

The Five watched with interest as Falcongate's best-known eccentric pushed to the front of the crowd and stood in front of Rowena Pruitt.

"Here," said Al Fresco Freddy, thrusting a flyer at the councillor. Ms Pruitt wrinkled her nose in disgust. "I'm starting a new business. Have a half-price coupon."

Max took a flyer as Freddy moved through the crowd. "Al Fresco Freddy Haulage," he read. "I carry coals to Newcastle."

"That's right!" Freddy shouted. He hopped up into a battered truck that was parked nearby. "I can't drive," he added, as he crunched the gears cheerfully, "but how hard can it be?"

The truck rocketed into reverse. The crowd scattered.

"Not hard!" Freddy roared in delight, mowing through the spectators. "Now if I could just learn how to stop!"

The truck was speeding towards the case containing the Falcongate Mariner. With a squeal, Ms Pruitt leaped out of its way. The truck hit the Mariner with an almighty crash, flipping it up into the air. The mummy came crashing down into the open truck as Freddy swerved up on to the pavement and off again.

The Five raced for their bikes. That mummy needed help!

Chapter Four

Al Fresco Freddy was still out of control. The kids pedalled hard to catch up.

"It's ridiculous," Dylan panted as he stood up in the saddle to get more speed. "Freddy gets to drive, and *I* can't see a 15-rated film."

Freddy veered off the road into a cornfield. "Run, corn!" he yelled. "Get out of me way! You're just standing there!"

Freddy was carving a corridor through the corn. The Five raced after him. If they could have seen the cornfield from the sky, they would have been very surprised to see the strange shapes they were marking out in the field.

At last, Freddy sped out of the field and on to a rough road. He bumped over a set of train tracks and threatened to disappear into the distance.

"We're never going to catch up with him . . ." Allie moaned as she leaned on her handlebars to get her breath back.

Almost as soon as the words were out of Allie's mouth, Freddy's truck snagged on a water pipe sticking out of the ground. The truck spun round as if it was on a turntable, and it was now heading straight towards the Kirrins.

Allie's eyes widened. "Though he could come back to us, which is very considerate . . ."

Jo spotted a pile of building materials and tools lying several metres from the edge of the train tracks: rails, spades, spare sleepers and a box of lethal-looking spikes for fixing them.

"Hey, Max," she said, nodding at the tools. "How are your railway-spike-throwing muscles shaping up?"

Max picked up the box and hurled its contents into the middle of the road. Spikes scattered everywhere. The Five cleared off the road at full speed, just as Freddy's truck roared over the spikes.

BANG! BANG!

The tyres exploded. Now the truck veered off the road completely. Freddy took a flying leap to the ground and landed in the arms of a surprised-looking scarecrow.

"Wahhh!" he yelled, giving the scarecrow a twirl. "Oh, you want to dance, eh? You're light on your feet."

With its tyres in ribbons, the truck backed into a haystack with a thud and stopped. The Kirrins raced to the truck and pulled the mummy case off the back.

"Is the Mariner hurt?" Allie asked anxiously.

Jo peered through the perspex. "He's fine," she said, taking deep breaths. "I mean, he's been dead for three thousand years, but other than that he's in great shape."

Back down on the beach, Max was again training for the Falcongate Junior Iron Man Competition.

"This is good exercise," Max panted as he strained to pedal his bike. A tow rope stretched out behind him. "But pulling the Mariner is a lot harder than I thought."

Dylan made himself more comfortable on top of the mummy's case, which was balanced on a small cart – which was tied to Max's bike.

"That's because there's a big lump shaped like Dylan on top of it," Jo said encouragingly.

The beach was now dotted with heavy trucks and tractors. Everywhere, vehicles were moving sand and digging trenches.

"Wow, you could build a pretty big sandcastle with all this stuff," Allie said, gazing around in awe.

Rupert Downpilt hurried over to them as fast as his short legs would allow.

"You found the Mariner!" he gasped, and clasped his hands together in delight. "He has come safe home, after his journey o'er the land and across Eternity!"

"Actually, we just dragged him down that hill and across a field," Jo said, thumbing behind her.

"We phoned the Town Hall, and they said you'd come back here," said Dylan.

Rupert Downpilt waved a sweaty hand at the digging equipment behind him. "To start digging," he said. "Councillor Pruitt kindly loaned me council machinery for the excavation."

Max leaned over to Downpilt. "If you find any alien landing gear shaped like a trapezium that glows orange and goes 'HHHHHWUUUUHHH!' could you let us know?" he asked.

Downpilt looked bewildered.

"It's all right," Jo assured the little archaeologist. "Sometimes we don't know what Max is talking about either."

Rupert Downpilt smiled weakly. "But . . . you children are heroes!" he said. "The world of archaeology is in your debt!" He flung his arms a little wider. "Your dog is . . . digging!"

Downpilt lowered his arms and stared at Timmy, who was digging enthusiastically in the sand near a rocky outcrop. "Why is he digging?" he said.

Jo shrugged. It was a pretty stupid question, in her opinion. "Because he's a dog," she said. "He's just digging in the sand."

"He could damage rare antiquities!" Downpilt gasped, looking less than pleased. "Get that mutt out of here!"

Retrieving an old tennis shoe from the hole, Timmy trotted over to Jo and dropped it at her feet. Jo picked up the shoe and handed it over to the

archaeologist. "Here's your rare antiquity," she said. "If you find the other one, the ancient Mariner can play tennis with you."

In George's study later that night, the Five watched the local news. It was a taped report from Falcongate's chief news reporter, Polly Lucas.

"This is Polly Lucas," said Polly Lucas from the beach where the Five had spent the afternoon, "reporting from Rupert Downpilt's excavation site."

The TV moved up half a metre. Jo, Allie, Dylan and Timmy's eyes moved with it.

"The big dig is already yielding exciting results . . ." Polly continued.

The TV sank down again.

"Max, stop doing squats with the TV," said Jo irritably, trying to keep the screen in her line of vision. "I want to see this."

Pausing mid-squat, Max held the TV very still. Polly Lucas was now interviewing Rupert Downpilt. The archaeologist was looking very excited.

"Near that rocky outcrop, Polly," said Downpilt breathlessly, "I've found what I'm certain are the foundations of an ancient grain storehouse."

The news camera panned across the "find". Stone foundations could clearly be seen lining the trenches.

"Imagine that!" Downpilt twittered. "Grain! In a storehouse! Mountains of grain!"

"Wait," said Jo suddenly. A familiar-looking rocky outcrop had just popped into view. "Those 'foundations' are exactly where Timmy was digging today."

Dylan frowned. "Yes, he was right near those rocks. Three hours ago, the only thing in that hole was an old tennis shoe." He looked at the others. "What's going on?"

It didn't make sense. Where had the foundations come from?

"Can I put the TV down now?" Max said in a strained voice. He shifted to get more comfortable. "I'm getting a giant cramp."

As Max put the TV down and rubbed his shoulders, something flickered in the dark woods that could just be seen from the study window. An orange glow . . . accompanied by a hissing roar . . .

Chapter Five

The sun had barely risen the next morning when the Five tramped across the woods towards the beach and the site of Rupert Downpilt's archaeological dig.

"I want to know how a grain storehouse that wasn't there in the afternoon was suddenly there last night," Jo said, shouldering her rucksack with determination.

The woods were thinning out. Now they all stopped and stared at a new chain-link fence closing off the beach. The Five stared at it, perplexed.

"The same way a fence that wasn't there

last night is suddenly here this morning," Dylan offered.

Following the fence, after a few hundred metres they came to a gate. As they approached it, a vision in dark blue uniform leaped out in front of them.

"Keeeeeee-uh-hhwwwaaaaaa . . ." Constable Stubblefield bellowed. She twirled her baton around her head, neck, shoulders and arms in a dazzling display of martial arts. "Oh, it's you young Kirrin types." She sniffed and tucked her baton into her belt. "Sorry, no admittance."

With a brisk nod, the constable walked several paces along the fence for a quick scout. By the time she walked back, the Kirrins were inside the gate.

"I *said* 'no admittance'!" said the police officer peevishly. "What part of 'Keeeeeee-uh-hhwwaaaa!' was ambiguous?"

"Oh, all right," Jo said, sounding almost as peevish as Constable Stubblefield. She cocked her head hopefully. "Er . . . has anyone reported seeing an orange glow in the woods at night?"

"And a sort of hissing roar?" Constable Stubblefield said. "Yes, various parties have reported such phenomena in various parts of the county."

She paced off along the fence again. The Five waited for her to return.

"We saw it in the woods by Otter Point!" Allie said once the police officer was back in earshot. "But we haven't been able to find it since then. Have you investigated?"

Constable Stubblefield waved her hand around the deserted beach. "Councillor Pruitt has me stuck here," she explained. She glanced left and right, and lowered her voice. "In addition, I avoid the woods at night," she said, "lest I find myself set upon by mischievous trolls."

The Five blinked as Constable Stubblefield straightened up again.

"Well, see you later," said Dylan, backing off. The others did the same. "If you're on patrol, I'm sure nobody's getting past you, Constable Stubblefield."

Everyone waved goodbye. The police officer waved back, then walked briskly down the fence again, checking left and right as she went.

"So," Dylan said to the others. "How are we getting past Constable Stubblefield?"

* * *

Needless to say, Jo had a plan. It wasn't her best plan. But even ridiculous plans worked some of the time.

Max had dressed up in a loose pirate shirt. He was holding Allie, dressed as a princess, in his arms. Jo fiddled with the focus on the digital camera as Dylan came up to Max with a small log. He wedged the log under Max's arm.

"Holding Allie was a good idea," said Max,

shifting his position. "She weighs a lot more than my barbells."

"Hey!" Allie protested.

Dylan tweaked the log until he was satisfied. "Well, this way you get exercise, *and* we end up with a way to get back on to the beach," he told Max.

Jo had fixed the focus. She pointed it at Max and Allie. "Say 'Stubblefield!'" she ordered, and took the photo. Then she handed the camera to Dylan, who plugged it into his laptop.

The picture of Max and Allie popped on to Dylan's screen. "Presto change-o," he murmured, clicking a few buttons, "Max becomes a pirate . . ."

Sure enough, Max's face suddenly sprouted long flowing hair and a pirate bandana.

"Allie becomes a princess," Dylan continued. "Bing . . . bing . . . bling . . ."

As he clicked on different parts of Allie's dress, glittering jewels appeared. Soon, Allie was encrusted with sparkles.

"And a log becomes a cannon," said Dylan with a final flourish, clicking on the log. It morphed into a ship's cannon as the others watched, open-mouthed.

Dylan hit the print button. The printer spewed out the doctored photo. Grinning broadly, Jo picked it up and waved it at the others. "And we have our Constable Stubblefield bait . . ." she said, and winked.

Chapter Six

Back on the beach that night, Constable Stubblefield was still on duty. She patrolled the fence, squinting at anything that moved. As she reached the excavation site, she peered through the fence. Rupert Downpilt's battered old camper van was parked on the edge of the site. The archaeologist was framed in the camper's window, leafing through a textbook.

"Stubblefield reports Downpilt in his camper van . . ." Constable Stubblefield reported into her hand-held tape recorder. "Stubblefield reports all clear to the south . . ."

Luckily, the Five weren't to the south. They were

hiding behind a nearby tree. Jo pulled a small battery-operated fan out of her pocket. Switching it on, she used it to waft a flyer along the ground. It fluttered to Stubblefield's feet and stopped.

The police officer picked up the flyer and studied it. Her eyes widened as she took in the photo of the heavily disguised Pirate Max and Princess Allie. "Fantastico at the Wolfsbridge Cinema signing autographs?!" she read aloud. She clutched at her chest. "Stubblefield reports heart palpitations!"

Duty was one thing. Romantic film heroes were something else.

"Don't worry, Fantastico – your delicate Stubblefield is on her way!" she warbled. And she skipped down the beach and out of sight.

The minute the coast was clear, the Five headed through the gate in the chain-link fence. As they walked past the camper van, the little archaeologist stepped outside. With seconds to spare, the cousins leaped behind a large dustbin a few metres from the van.

Rupert Downpilt was carrying an overflowing wastepaper basket. He tipped it into the dustbin,

then wiped his hands down his overalls. The cousins cringed back, out of sight. Timmy sniffed at something that had missed the dustbin and now lay on the ground. With his nose still deep in his book, Rupert Downpilt didn't notice.

As soon as Downpilt had returned to his camper van, the Five stepped out of their hiding place. Their hearts were beating like drums. Timmy nosed at Jo's hand, and pressed the thing he'd found into her palm.

"Look at this – another salami wrapper," said Jo, studying the piece of plastic that Timmy had given her. "Just like we found in the woods."

"And did you notice Downpilt's overalls?" Dylan put in. "The legs were all singed. Like the grass in the clearing."

Allie looked over at a new set of trenches. "And what's going on *here*?" she said, putting her hands on her hips.

Downpilt's excavation was moving fast. Long trenches had been laid out on a grid. The lines were staked and marked with string. The contents of the trenches were particularly interesting. They contained stone foundations, ancient steps

and several bits of upright wall.

"It almost looks like when they built a huge mall back home," said Allie, gazing around. She gave a little shiver. "Sorry," she explained to the others. "I get goose bumps when I think of shopping."

"I assume your mall didn't have a giant granite wheel for grinding grain," said Jo.

A huge stone wheel lay in one of the trenches. Balanced on its edge, the wheel was attached to a wooden post in the centre of a round, flat surface.

"No," Allie agreed. "But it had a store that sold jewellery for cats . . ."

Something didn't smell right about this place.

"I still don't get it," Jo said with a frown. "This is right where Timmy was digging – this *wasn't here* before."

Max shrugged. "Maybe not, but it makes a great obstacle course now."

Unable to resist the challenge, Max jumped in and out of a few trenches like a kangaroo. He jogged over to a set of stone steps and ran up and down a dozen times. Then he stopped, punched the air and did a triumphant little jig. Inevitably, he lost his balance and fell down the steps on his backside.

"Once again – Plan B," Dylan crowed, pointing. "Fall on your bum."

The Five had their backs to the grinding-stone. They didn't see a gloved hand removing the pin which attached the stone to the central post. The wheel wobbled, fell off, landed on its edge and started rolling straight towards the cousins.

Timmy saw the danger first. He barked a warning.

"I suggest Plan C – run!" Jo ordered, backing away from the stone as fast as she could.

The others obeyed instantly. The huge stone wheel was gathering speed. It knocked into several wheelbarrows laden with spades and pick-axes. The air was filled with flying blades, forcing the kids to duck and dodge as they ran.

"Can that wheel run over us?" Allie squealed, throwing herself to one side as a sharp-looking spade hurtled over her head.

"No problem," Dylan panted. "There's a wall in its way."

Allie dived the other way as the wheel bore down on the wall Dylan had spotted. It smashed through it as if the wall was made of cardboard.

Now there were melon-sized balls flying through the air as well. In the nick of time, Allie and Dylan flung themselves into a trench and covered their heads. The stones flew over them and smashed into a wooden shed nearby. The shed groaned and collapsed, covering Allie and Dylan's trench completely.

"See," Dylan said a little weakly as Max started digging them out. "No problem."

The grinding-stone was still rolling. Now it was heading for Jo and Timmy. They backed towards a narrow alley of parked diggers and dumper trucks, turned and sprinted between the vehicles. But it was no good. The grinding-stone was closing the gap.

"In here, Timmy!" Jo yelled, seizing one of the site wheelbarrows and turning it upside-down.

She and Timmy crouched down under their metal umbrella as the grinding-stone thundered towards them. It moved up the slope of the upturned wheelbarrow like a ramp, flew through the air and smacked into a set of foundations in a nearby trench. There was a dull crack as the foundation stones broke in half. The grinding-stone

ran out of steam and fell harmlessly on its side in the sand.

Jo clambered out from beneath the wheelbarrow. Timmy crept out very carefully behind her. "I don't know about you lot," she said, getting her breath back as the others raced over, "but I find it odd that that wheel just started rolling on its own."

Dylan pointed at the cracked foundation stones. "Well, this is pretty odd, too," he said. "This looks like granite on the outside, but . . ." he bent down and took a handful of the white stuff inside the shattered stones, ". . . it's kind of rubbery plaster inside."

"Granite outside, rubbery plaster inside." Max shook his head. "That would make a really bad pastry."

Jo took a handful of the white stuff and ran it through her fingers. "Well, whatever this stuff is, it didn't exist in the Bronze Age," she said.

Timmy trotted up with one of the stones from the shattered wall in his mouth. He dropped it on the foundation, and it cracked open like an egg.

"This 'rock' is made of the same stuff," Allie gasped. "What's Downpilt up to?"

Chapter Seven

The Five all looked towards Rupert Downpilt's camper van.

"He eats salami," Jo said, ticking things off on her fingers, "and his clothes were singed, so he must have something to do with that roar and glow we saw the other night."

"So let's follow his camper van," Dylan suggested. "I bet that's where tonight's roar and glow will happen."

"How can we keep up with the camper van?" Allie asked.

"Timmy can tell us where it goes," Dylan said promptly. "Max, give me your T-shirt."

Max looked confused. He pulled off his shirt and handed it over to Dylan. Dylan stuck it under Timmy's nose. The dog made a face and sneezed violently.

"I know – Max needs to shower after he exercises," Dylan agreed, patting Timmy sympathetically. "We can smell him a mile off." Motioning to the others, he crept towards the camper van, where he tied the shirt to the van's rear bumper. "But *Timmy* can smell him from *ten* miles off . . ." he added with a grin.

When the sun had set, the Five returned to the excavation site. There was still no sign of Constable Stubblefield. There was also no sign of Rupert Downpilt's camper van.

Timmy sniffed the place where the van had been parked. Then he shot off towards the woods that fringed the beach. The Kirrins followed him, leaping over rocks and tussocks and sand dunes. Timmy surged on, into the woods and through the trees.

After a fifteen-minute chase, the dog stopped, pricked his ears and sat completely still. The kids crept up beside him, and peered through the trees.

The camper van was parked in a clearing just ahead of them. The hatch at the back was open, revealing a portable workshop of some kind. Downpilt was bent over a trapezium-shaped kiln that had been placed on the grass. He was stoking the kiln's hissing fire.

The Kirrins watched as the archaeologist stirred a mixture in a bucket that stood on a nearby work table. He picked up the bucket and poured its contents into an oar-shaped mould. The thick

liquid hissed and spread. Downpilt then pulled something from the kiln with his gloved hands. With a practised motion, he popped a crude water jug out of the mould and set it down to cool.

"Hello, 'mysterious orange glow'," Jo murmured, watching. "That's where all the 'ruins' come from. He made them and put them there."

"He's turning out more fake stuff than a Beverly Hills plastic surgeon," Allie said.

Dylan frowned as he worked it out. "So the entire excavation is fake, and he's using it to close down the whole coast!" he said.

"We can't tell Stubblefield right now," said Allie, looking worried. "She's on her way to see Fantastico."

The kids got into a huddle. They needed a strategy before Downpilt went any further with his dastardly plan.

"We've got to tell *someone* what's going on," Max said at last. "We should find Councillor Pruitt."

"Found her," Dylan said grimly.

The others spun round. Councillor Rowena Pruitt was stepping into the clearing. From the way she greeted Downpilt, it was clear that they were in on this together.

"Our grand project marches forward," Pruitt twittered, clapping her hands and snorting out another of her giggles. "Hip-hip-hooray."

"Did you bring the final blueprints?" Downpilt demanded.

"They're hidden in my office," said Councillor Pruitt soothingly. "I tried to bring them to the site earlier, but there were some kids snooping about."

Rupert Downpilt looked furious. "Kids? Snooping? I don't like kids snooping! *No snooping!*"

"Not to worry," said Councillor Pruitt. "I chased them off with the grinding wheel. Can't have anyone figuring out this is all fake."

The Five listened to Councillor Pruitt's snorting laughter with dismay.

"How are we going to report them to the authorities?" Allie wailed. "She is the authorities!"

A pine cone fell from a tree above the Five. It landed on the ground with a thud.

"What was that?" said Rupert Downpilt, swinging round and staring at the dark patch of trees where the Five were hiding. "Who's over there?"

Chapter Eight

The Five stood frozen to the spot as Rupert
Downpilt and Rowena Pruitt ran towards them.
They hadn't been seen – yet.

"You weren't followed, were you?" Rupert
Downpilt hissed at his accomplice.

In desperation, Jo put her hands to her mouth.
She did a perfect bird call, imitating a crow.

Rowena Pruitt stopped at once. "Ah, it's just a
crow," she said, flapping her hand at Downpilt. She
turned back towards the kiln and the camper van.
"You fret too much."

Dylan picked up another pine cone. He threw it
as hard as he could to the far side of the clearing.

Councillor Pruitt's head snapped round as though it was on elastic.

"What was *that?*" she gasped.

Pruitt and Downpilt rushed off in the opposite direction, away from the Five. Seizing their opportunity, the kids and Timmy scampered away. It had been a close call.

They wasted no time. Within half an hour, the Five were standing outside the Town Hall.

"We know *what* Pruitt and Downpilt are doing," said Jo, looking up at the windows.

"And we know where," said Max. "And how and when."

Jo walked round to the side of the Town Hall and back again. "So if we can get into Pruitt's office," she said, trying a couple of windows, "maybe we can find out why."

Dylan prodded his cousin. "Max, I think the Junior Iron Man banner there might come in handy."

He pointed to a banner hanging across the street. It featured Olympian-looking figures of a swimmer, a cyclist and a runner. The Iron Man

competition meant being able to do all three activities, one after the other. The banner was strung high up, from a lamp post on the far side of the street over to the Town Hall itself.

Max looked at his biceps and gave them a quick flex. "OK, muscles," he instructed them. "Do your stuff."

He ran to the lamp post and started climbing, hand over hand. When he reached the banner, he swung along like a monkey, pausing about halfway.

"Phew," he gasped, adjusting his grip. "Some of this stuff's more tiring than it looks."

Max moved on along the banner. He reached the roof of the Town Hall. Then he scampered over to a skylight and tested it. It was unlocked. Max flung it open, gave his watching cousins the thumbs-up, and dropped through the hole.

The others heard a thump and a bounce. Max's silhouette flew past the topmost window, landing in what looked like a wheeled office chair. The chair rolled out of sight. Jo, Allie and Dylan watched as the chair and Max bumped and thumped their way through a series of rooms and down a couple of stairwells.

When Max reached the bottom floor, the chair ground to a halt. Standing up and dusting himself down, he headed for the front door and opened it to let the others in.

"That was fun," he panted. "And I got a bit of rest while I was at it."

Finding Councillor Pruitt's office wasn't difficult. Luckily, the door was unlocked.

"All right," said Jo, looking around. "If you were blueprints, where would you be?"

Everyone started searching. They made their way through the desk and the large filing cabinet. They checked under the sofa. They checked behind pictures, under the carpet and in the wastepaper basket. At last, Allie crossed to a brass coat rack that stood in the corner of the office. She pulled the knob on top. The knob came off in her hands, revealing the blueprints.

The others were amazed.

"I always find my Christmas presents early, too," Allie explained as she unrolled the blueprints for everyone to see.

"That's our beach," Dylan said, pointing to a section of the blueprint. He frowned. "But . . . these

blueprints are for a luxury resort hotel."

"Look – the building plans match where they've dug all the trenches," Max gasped.

"Ooh look – they have an infinity pool!" Allie squealed, rather missing the point. "And cabanas!"

"I'm so pleased you approve," said Rowena Pruitt.

The Five whirled round. Pruitt and Downpilt were standing at the door. The councillor gave another one of her horrible giggles.

Jo knew the best form of defence was attack. "So the whole ancient fishing village thing is just so you can get control of the beach, build a resort hotel and get rich!" she accused.

"Well, rich . . ." Dylan began, trying to be fair. Jo glared at him. "Sorry," he mumbled, and fell quiet.

"That's right," said Rupert Downpilt defiantly. The tools around his belt tinkled. "Pruitt's giving me the land to build a museum dedicated to the excavation."

"And then I bet you'll 'discover' that the site isn't ancient at all – just some old camping ground or something," Jo said in disgust.

"And after that, you'll cancel the museum plan and turn it into your hotel," Max finished.

Downpilt's eyes narrowed. "Now that you know, we can't have you telling anybody . . ." he said.

And he started moving towards them with a dangerous look on his face.

Chapter Nine

Half an hour later, the Five were back at the beach. They walked along the cliff, closely followed by Downpilt and Rowena Pruitt.

"We want this to look like an accident," said Rowena Pruitt cheerfully. She prodded Max in the back to hurry him along. "Nothing to link it to us. Hip-hip-hooray."

"I've got to hand it to you, Councillor Pruitt – you outsmarted us," said Dylan admiringly.

The others glanced round. What was Dylan up to?

"I suppose we really needed a Plan B," Dylan said meaningfully.

They had stumbled on a few more paces before Jo clicked. "Yes, Plan B!" she shouted. *"Now!"*

The Five dropped on to their bottoms. Downpilt and Pruitt stumbled and tripped over them.

"Woahhhhhh!"

"This is not dignified!" Rowena Pruitt wailed as she struggled to her feet.

Paying no heed to the floundering villains, the kids slid down the cliff on their bottoms.

"Plan B – sliding down on bum!" Allie squealed as she took a bumpy corner down to the beach. She spotted a cave hidden in the rocks. There wasn't a moment to lose. "Quick – in here!" she yelled to the others, scrambling to her feet and running across the sand towards the cave.

Everyone swerved into the cave after Allie. They switched on their torches. The beams illuminated a large stone chamber.

"We can hide while we figure out our next move," Allie explained.

It was a good suggestion. But it hadn't taken Downpilt and Pruitt's next move into account. The Five heard a stone scraping across the entrance and swung round. The cave mouth was already almost

51

sealed by the grinding-stone that had so recently chased them across the beach. Puffing with exertion, Downpilt and Pruitt wedged the stone into place with two rocks. This time, it wasn't rolling anywhere.

"There!" Downpilt yelled through the tiny crack of daylight that remained. "It may be fake, but it's very heavy."

"A hundred years from now, *you'll* be an archaeological find!" Rowena Pruitt snorted.

The Five rushed towards the stone slab. They pushed against it with all their strength. It was impossible to put any real pressure on the stone with the sandy floor slipping about under their feet.

"Wooahhh!" they yelled, and pitched together into a heap.

"Well," Jo said, from somewhere underneath Dylan. "It looks like our next move is slowly starving in here."

Water trickled down on to Dylan's head. "And getting rained on while we wait," Dylan grumbled, looking up. Another drop splashed into his eye. "Where's that water coming from?"

Everyone shone their torches at the cave roof.

They saw a tiny opening. Water was draining through it.

"Must be waves breaking on the rocks," Max guessed. "Too bad we can't get up there."

The others looked at him.

"What?" Max asked.

All of Max's Junior Iron Man training was going to be needed for this one. Dylan and Jo stood side-by-side on the damp sand. Allie balanced on their shoulders. Pulling himself up their backs, Max at

last stood on Allie's shoulders. He reached up for the cave roof.

"I can just barely reach through the hole," he gasped, feeling for the opening. "I don't know if I can pull myself up."

Scraping around for a handhold, Max knocked some pebbles and dirt loose. They fell into Allie's face. Allie coughed, wobbled – and lost her balance.

"Whoa!"

Allie tumbled off Jo and Dylan's shoulders, knocking them down as well.

"Ooooff!"

Now Max was dangling from the cave roof by his fingertips. Without the others, it was a long way down. "Well," he panted. "That gives me some incentive."

He struggled to heave himself up through the hole. Timmy barked encouragingly. With one last almighty effort, Max pulled himself up and got his knees on the rock face. He wriggled through the gap and was gone.

Max was back on the rocks that they had just slid down. He headed down towards the beach,

checking for Downpilt and Pruitt as he went. But they were long gone.

As soon as he reached the beach, he ran towards the huge grinding-stone blocking the cave mouth.

"Rock . . ." he panted, kicking away the two rocks that held the stone in place. ". . . and roll!"

The grinding-stone didn't move.

"Not rolling . . ." said Max in disappointment. He studied the slab. Then he took a deep breath and tried pushing. Still nothing.

With an immense effort and a very red face, Max put his shoulder into the stone and shoved with all his might. The grinding-stone moved very slightly. But it was just enough for the others to squeeze through the gap.

Max collapsed on the beach as his cousins flooded around him. He was utterly exhausted.

"There," Dylan said cheerfully. "That wasn't so hard, was it?"

"There were . . . two of them . . . One of me . . ." Max improvised. "Told you I was tired. Just need . . . to catch my – whooaa!"

Jo had grabbed him and pulled him back on to his feet. There was no time for a rest.

"Come on!" she shouted.

And as usual, the others followed.

Chapter Ten

Having got rid of the pesky kids, Downpilt and Pruitt were back at the archaeologist's camper van.

"Here will be the Outdoor Massage and Sushi Pavilion," said Rowena Pruitt proudly, pointing at the blueprints on the table. "Hip-hip-hooray!"

Both villains jumped out of their skin at the sound of rapping on the windscreen. Jo was pressing her face to the glass, mouth open, cheeks inflated and her eyes bugging out of her head. It was pretty funny.

Councillor Pruitt's eyes bugged in their turn. "She's mocking us!" she shouted, slamming the blueprints down and racing for the side door of the

camper van. Dignity was a big thing with the councillor. "I will not be mocked!"

Jo slid away into the shadows as Pruitt and Downpilt rushed out of the camper van and on to the beach. Dylan stood several metres away.

"Hey!" he yelled through his cupped hands. "Archaeology is stupid!"

Rupert Downpilt looked enraged. "It is not!" he roared.

Both villains hurried towards Dylan, intent on catching him. They weren't looking where they were going. Stepping on to a large tarpaulin that had been stretched across the sand, they both fell into a chest-deep hole.

"Ahh – woahhhhhh!"

A magnificent chain of events began to unfurl. As the tarpaulin collapsed beneath Pruitt and Downpilt, a rope tied to one corner was pulled. The rope had been tethered to a wedge, which held one of the site wheelbarrows secure – contents and all. The wheelbarrow was secure no more. The whistling rope tugged the wedge away. The barrow rolled down a ramp and crashed into one of Downpilt's lovingly moulded "stone" pillars. There

was a groaning sound as the pillar toppled over, taking out another pillar on its way – which took out another – and another.

The last pillar in the row had a spade tied to the top. As the pillar toppled, the sharp digging edge of the spade sliced through a taut rope running up to a small crane. At the top of the crane dangled the Falcongate Mariner's empty case.

"Oh," Rowena Pruitt moaned as the case began to fall. "My dignity is going to suffer."

With perfect accuracy, the perspex case – open end first – fell down on top of Pruitt and Downpilt. They were trapped like a pair of stuffed badgers.

"Ohhhhh," they moaned, bashing at their plastic prison. "Owwwwww!"

"Hip-hip-hooray," said Max, Jo, Allie and Dylan in unison, throwing in a perfect impression of Councillor Pruitt's snorty laugh at the end.

"Woof!" Timmy added.

"Let us out of here!" Rowena Pruitt snorted as the kids gathered round their catch. "Let me free! Oh . . ."

Timmy growled and she fell back in defeat.

"Here, let me try . . ." Max said insincerely. He

prodded the case with one finger. "Sorry," he said, taking his finger away. "Way too tired. I am, actually," he told the others, swaying on his feet. "I'm going to sit down."

Jo waved her hand around. "Stretch out," she invited. "It's *our* beach again."

With a wop-wop of sirens, Constable Stubblefield's squad car squealed to a halt beside the mummy's case. Red-faced and angry, the police officer leaped out.

"There *was* no Fantastico!" she said furiously. "Wild goose chase!" She did a double-take at Downpilt and Pruitt. "What are *they* doing?" she said.

"They're regretting that they made a fake archaeological site so they could use the whole coast for a resort hotel," said Jo cheerfully.

Constable Stubblefield's face turned redder. "This whole thing was a *fake*?!" she roared. She spotted the fake Mariner propped up against Downpilt's camper van. "The *Mariner* was a fake?!" she roared even more loudly. "And Pruitt made me guard it in my free time?! *I missed my autoharp lesson!*"

The police officer grabbed the Mariner in fury

and slammed it down on the ground, stamping on it for good measure.

"On second thoughts," Downpilt said nervously as the police constable whirled her arms around in deadly fashion, almost severing the Mariner's head from its neck, "I think we'll stay in here."

The Falcongate Iron Man competition began the following day. Half a dozen kids stood on the start line, limbering up quietly. Max stood among them. He still looked exhausted from his exertions the day before.

"Max looks really sleepy," said Allie, as she and the others watched from the sidelines. "I hope he'll be competitive."

Constable Stubblefield stepped up to the start line. She pulled out her starter's pistol. "Junior Iron Man competitors," she shouted, "take your marks!"

BANG!

The competitors took off down the street. Max wobbled a few steps, turned round and lurched slowly in the opposite direction.

"Define 'competitive'," said Jo.

Allie and Dylan ran after Max.

"Max! Max!" Dylan shouted as his cousin weaved along. "You're running the wrong way!"

"I'm running the right way," Max said woozily, brushing Dylan and Allie away. "I'm going home and back to bed."

He headed on, slowly and wonkily. His duvet was calling. The others looked at each other, shrugged and ran after him. Timmy barked alongside them the whole way.

Home sounded good to them.

Epilogue

Allie and Jo took up their positions in the sand as Dylan got the videocamera into place on his shoulder.

"Sticky Situation Number Twelve," said Dylan, raising his voice above the swoosh of the waves on the beach. "You Need To Excavate A Bog Man."

"You never know when you're going to come across prehistoric remains that you want to excavate," said Jo, looking up into the camera lens.

"But you have to be careful," Allie added. "You don't use picks and shovels, you use nail files and paintbrushes." She held up these tools, just in case the viewers had no idea what she was talking about.

"Because you don't want to hurt the fossils," Jo continued. She looked down at where she and Allie were digging. "Or, in our case, Max," she added, "because we don't have a real Bog Man."

Dylan zoomed in to where Max's blond head was sticking out of the sand.

"Hello," Max said cheerfully. He would have waved, but his hands were buried.

"Being ever so careful, you clear away the dirt and debris," Jo said.

She and Allie bent over their task. A few moments' delicate brushing, and they had revealed Max's big toe.

"Stop it!" Max giggled, wriggling helplessly. "You're tickling me!"

There was a sandy explosion as Max burst out of the ground and ran down into the water.

"Of course," Allie said, brushing herself down, "it helps if your prehistoric remains aren't ticklish."

Max was now leaping around in the waves like an excitable dolphin.

"Woaah!" Allie and Jo squealed, running out to join their cousin in the water.

Dylan sighed, set down the camera and ran out as well.

There's only so much filming you can do before something else comes along that is *much* more fun.

THE CASE OF THE
GOBBLING GOOP

Look out for the next
Famous 5 Case File . . .

Hodder
Children's
Books

A division of Hachette Children's Books

The
Famous Five's
SURVIVAL GUIDE

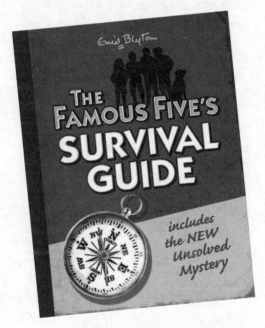

Packed with useful information on surviving outdoors and solving mysteries, here is the one mystery that the Famous Five never managed to solve. See if you can follow the trail to discover the location of the priceless Royal Dragon of Siam.

The perfect book for all fans of mystery, adventure and the Famous Five!

ISBN 9780340970836

Read the adventures of George and the
original Famous Five in